Brown
Paper Bear

For Eve, Marcus and Leon

First published in paperback in 2005
First published in 2004 by Macmillan Children's Books
A division of Macmillan Publishers Limited
20 New Wharf Road, London N1 9RR
Basingstoke and Oxford
Associated companies throughout the world
www.panmacmillan.com

Produced by Fernleigh Books
1A London Road, Enfield
Middlesex EN2 6BN

ISBN 1 405 05085 3

1 3 5 7 9 8 6 4 2

A CIP catalogue record for this book is available
from the British Library.

Manufactured in China.

Brown Paper Bear

Illustrated by Neil Reed

MACMILLAN CHILDREN'S BOOKS

Jess had never stayed at Grandad's on her own before. She was sleeping in the room that had been his when he was a little boy, but now the room was very bare. Jess wished she had brought some of her toys from home. There was nothing here for her to play with – and she didn't like being alone in the dark.

But at last her eyes closed, and Jess fell fast asleep.

Suddenly, Jess heard a creak. She opened her eyes.
A bright shaft of moonlight was streaming through
the curtains and shining onto an open cupboard.
It was a cupboard she had never noticed before.

Through the cobwebs, Jess could see odd dusty
shapes: an old tennis racquet, some building blocks . . .
and a squashy brown paper parcel tied with red ribbon.
Jess reached for the parcel. The ribbon was knotted, and she
struggled to undo it. But inside was a wonderful surprise.

It was a teddy bear.

One ear was coming loose, and his fur had worn rather thin in places, but the bear was the warm, soft colour of brown paper, and his eyes shone.

"He could almost be alive," thought Jess.

Suddenly, she felt the bear start to wriggle in her arms. Then he spoke.

Jess stared.

"Hello, Jess," said the bear. "I belonged to your grandfather when he was a little boy. But he got too old to play with me, and put me away in the cupboard. I've been there ever since."

"I'm glad I found you," smiled Jess. "Now I'll have someone to play with." And she reached out to take his paw.

As her hand touched the bear's fur, Jess felt a strange tingling. Then, in a sudden rush of air, she felt herself flying through the sky.

"Hold on tight, we're going higher!" sang out the bear, as they flew up above the fields and out over the moonlit sea. Jess laughed in delight.

All too soon, the journey was over. Jess and the bear floated back down to earth and in through an open window.

The room seemed strangely familiar . . . but Jess had never seen such toys! They were rather old-fashioned, but bright, and shining like new.

"Come and meet my friends!" said the bear.

The bear introduced Jess to all the other toys. The Jack-in-a-box gave her a big surprise!

"And this is Captain Smart," said the bear proudly.

"At your service, Ma'am!" shouted a tall soldier with a shiny black moustache. "Would you like to join our parade?"

"Oh, yes please," said Jess, and she and the bear fell in behind the last soldier.

They all marched up and down, swinging their arms. Jess was having a lovely time!

Then they caught sight of a shiny green toy train.
"Come on, Jess," cried the bear. "I'll be the guard, and
you can be the driver!"

So they all clambered on board and the train set off to race
around the room – under the table, and past the doll's house.
What a ride they had!

"Phew! That was fun!" said Jess, as the train came to a halt. Then something knocked her off her feet.

"Down, boy!" called the bear sternly. "That dog needs to learn some manners!"

But Percy the Puppy was sitting on Jess, licking her and wagging his tail.

"Stop!" giggled Jess. "I'm all wet!" And she tickled the puppy until he jumped off.

"And now may I present Miss Betsy," said the bear.
The beautiful china doll curtseyed to the floor. Then she asked sweetly, "Will you dance with me, Jess?"
Soft tinkling music filled the air, and Jess and Miss Betsy danced a graceful waltz.

Jess was still spinning and floating when she felt
a sharp tweak on her ear. It was Toby the monkey.
  "Come and play with me now," he said, and jumped
over a building block.
  "Hey, you cheeky thing!" cried Jess. And she chased
him all around the room.

But at last it was time to go.
Jess said goodbye to all her new friends,
and thanked them for such a special night.
"Goodbye!" called the toys. "Come back soon!"
Then, hand in paw, Jess and
the bear flew home.

"Why, Jess, you've found my old teddy bear,"
said Grandad next morning. "I thought
I'd lost him long ago."
Jess smiled. "Now he's my
friend, too," she said. "My very
own brown paper bear."